MERRY CHRISTMAS, HENRY

A CHICAGO CHRISTMAS #1

AUBREY WYNNE OWNER

Editing by The Editing Hall, Sherry Merry

Cover Art by Imagination Uncovered, Taylor Sullivan

ISBN: 978-0-9971841-3-6

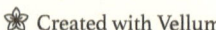 Created with Vellum

DEDICATION

To Danny, my loving husband and Rock of Gibraltar. To Mindy, my sister, best friend, and constant muse.

Merry Christmas, Henry

Winner of the Preditor and Editors Reader's Choice Short Story Award:

Merry Christmas, Henry 2013

"Aubrey Wynne creates a character that's easy to fall in love with..."

~Kishan Paul, author of Blind Love and Second Wife

"Captivating Christmas Choice!"

~Kindle Book Review

SUMMARY

Merry Christmas, Henry

Henry, a shy and talented artist, moonlights as a security guard at a museum and loses his heart to a beautiful, melancholy woman in a painting. As his obsession grows, he finds a kindred soul who helps him in his search for happiness. On Christmas Eve, Henry dares to take a chance on love and fulfill his dream.

1

"The museum will be closing in five minutes. Please make your way to the nearest exit."

Henry tore his gaze from the painting, and looked around at the weekend crowd hurrying by. No one noticed him. He always blended into the background. Henry the Trifling—that would have been the title of his self-portrait. A soft sigh escaped as he pulled his gray coat over the frayed cuffs of a cotton shirt. There were extraordinary people and there were ordinary people. Henry considered himself less than ordinary. He was insignificant.

"You'll never amount to nothin'. Just like your worthless father."

He shrugged off the memory of his mother's nagging image and looked toward the last group of art enthusiasts headed in his direction.

This was his favorite part of the day. In a crush of people, everyone was equal. No one stood out in the sea of indistinguishable faces. There was no pressure to make witty or charming conversation. Henry liked people but had never been good at interaction. The anonymity of a crowd gave the illusion of belonging. For a man as painfully shy as Henry, it was the only way to mingle in a city like Chicago.

Casting a last wistful look at the lady in the painting, Henry took a deep breath and eased into the middle of the exiting crowd. A large woman trying to grab her boisterous child knocked into his left shoulder. She distractedly patted a chubby hand at the obstruction and mumbled a quick apology without glancing his way. Henry smiled and nodded.

The group approached the turnstile and bunched up, shoulder to shoulder, waiting for their turn to leave. Someone jostled him from the side and he felt the heat of another body against his back. He tried to absorb the vivid energy surrounding him. Last week a pretty woman had smiled at him. He had felt warm all the way home. He'd started painting her but had not yet decided on the setting. It had to be somewhere as beautiful and inviting as her smile—Venice, perhaps.

Stepping onto the sidewalk, he buttoned his overcoat against the early November chill. Christmas lights intermingled with the traffic lights, blinking and glowing on the wet streets. The wind had picked up and people rushed by with their heads down. Henry pulled his collar up against the icy sting of a light rain and quickly walked the few blocks to his small apartment.

Stopping in front of the dilapidated building, Henry looked up at his fourth floor window. He always left the light on so it seemed as if someone was home to greet him. He smiled as his thoughts returned to the woman in the painting. He would never forget that snowy December day she arrived at the museum. He had been working his usual graveyard shift and the day manager had needed help with a shipment arriving that morning.

"Hey, Henry, you want a little overtime?" the supervisor had asked. "Charlie called in sick and I could use an extra hand. Another rich collector remembered us in his will. We've got a pricey piece arriving in about an hour and I'd feel better with some extra security."

Henry tried to wipe the smile off his face. Five years in the city and he still felt like a country bumpkin. "Sure."

"The paper says a Rubens. Flemish, wasn't he? But it's a small one."

Henry gave a whistle. "Impressive."

"There's a companion painting with it, artist unknown. We'll have to find a spot for it in appreciation for the collector's piece."

An hour later, Henry held a priceless painting in his hands. God, he loved this job.

"The family probably figured they wouldn't get any money out of the other one. But this one sure is a beauty," the supervisor said as he reached for the Rubens.

"Yes, indeed," Henry replied, as his eyes landed on the second painting. "Striking."

Henry's boss laughed. "I'm talking about this one, Bud. The little one is worth the big bucks!" His boss headed toward the office to start the paperwork on the new museum pieces.

"Yes, of course," he murmured, but his attention remained focused on the woman in the larger painting.

She sat on the edge of a rocky cliff, her face slightly turned as if looking over the edge. Her legs were out to the side, knees bent, a long, olive-colored skirt spread around her haphazardly as if blown by the wind. The stormy ocean breakers rushed between jagged rocks then turned into frothy waves that lapped at the sand. The details in the picture were crisp and stark, the color was minimal—just the woman on a cliff with the turbulent water below. But the overall effect created a hauntingly beautiful scene.

He felt her distress, her sorrow. His fingers itched to reach out and pull her from the painting and hold her, soothe her, give her comfort. Henry knew that if she could turn and face him, he would be looking at the most exquisite creature he'd ever seen. His hand shook as he reached out to touch the canvas.

"Are you okay, Henry?"

Henry drew his hand back quickly as if he'd been caught in the act of—of what? Touching a frame? Good lord, he must be tired.

"What? Oh, yeah, I just need some sleep. " As Henry turned to leave, he took one last look at the woman who had just stolen his heart. Fate had given him a precious gift. He whistled "Angels We Have Heard on High" all the way home.

The woman soon became an obsession. For the next ten years, he spent his lunch breaks in front of her portrait— occasionally even talking to her. Not that he expected her to respond—it was just nice to think she was listening. She conveyed a gentle melancholy that beckoned to him, a kindred soul of sorts.

Now, when he looked at the light in his window, he imagined her waiting for him in the kitchen with a pot of soup on the stove and a warm loaf of bread just out of the oven. Rebecca, as he had come to call her, would welcome him with a smile and a light kiss, and then ask about his day.

He took the steps of the old tenant building two at a time and checked mailbox Number Fourteen. Flipping through junk mail and bills, he climbed the four flights to his door. His aunt never missed his birthday or holidays, and Thanksgiving was coming up. He should get a card for that.

It was at the bottom of the pile. He recognized Aunt Lucy's flamboyant scrawl at once. Her signature rosewater scent drifted from the envelope as he tore open the back. He grinned as he thought of how strong the perfume must be to survive the trip all the way from New York City. His aunt never did anything in a small way.

Henry appreciated the handwritten note she always included with the latest news. Throughout the years, she had kept him informed of her family's everyday happenings. Her descriptions of events like the kids' bout with chicken pox, Jason's first date, and Lisa's debut behind the wheel of a car had made him laugh out loud. Although he had only met her husband and children a handful of times, the frequent letters made him feel part of their family.

Digging the keys out of his jeans pocket, he unlocked the door and dumped the mail, except for Aunt Lucy's card, on the hall table. As he walked into the living room, his transformation was immediate. Taking in a deep breath, Henry smiled as the smell of oil paint and kerosene filled his nostrils. The large room exploded with color, chasing away all thoughts of the dreary weather outside. He looked around at the walls crowded with his paintings and felt a deep satisfaction. Frames of various sizes were hung haphazardly wherever there was a space big enough to fit them. The portraits were of people—in the park, along the shores of Lake Michigan, on a mountain in the Alps.

The corner loft apartment was an ideal location for Henry. Working midnights at the museum, he needed to sleep through the morning or grab an occasional nap in the evening. The top floor made that possible. With windows facing the south and west, the room was filled with natural light. Henry spent almost every afternoon painting. His longtime friend Melinda called it "his work," but that made it sound like a chore.

The job as a security guard paid the bills. His painting gave him purpose. This was his sanctuary and refuge from the hectic world outside. As he walked into the room, the slump in his shoulders gave way to an energy that lent a confidence to his movements. A gleam appeared in his ebony eyes. The silver in his black, collar-length hair gave him an air of sophistication rather than age.

A woman meeting him for the first time here, in his own territory, would find him attractive. She would meet Hank, the talented artist who could look into people's souls and bring them alive on canvas. She would never connect him to Henry, the shy, inconspicuous museum employee.

He headed for one of the many collections of paintings stacked against the walls. He quickly flipped past the first few, wood thumping against wood, and found the one he wanted. Setting it up on the windowsill, he stepped back, folded his arms, and considered the piece.

Merry Christmas, Melinda, he thought, as he took off his coat and hung it on the coat stand in the hallway.

He sank into the cushions of his favorite chair and rubbed his palms against the worn, woven material as he studied his life's accomplishments. Behind the frames were dingy walls and faded paint, but Hank never saw past the canvas. Yes, he could afford a nicer place, but it just didn't seem worth the effort to move. Besides, he was so close to the museum—and her.

His gaze wandered to the painting of his aunt and her family when her kids were young. Henry had copied it from an old photo taken during one of their rare visits to Chicago and painted them into a Christmas scene. It was an idyllic portrait and exactly the way he hoped Aunt Lucy's life had turned out.

Hank pulled out the Thanksgiving card with a silly looking cartoon turkey on the front and read the sentimental Hallmark saying on the inside with a snort. Then he opened the neatly folded letter from Aunt Lucy.

"Dear Hank," it began. He scanned the beginning, which said she hoped he was doing well and asked her usual array of questions. "Are you getting out?" "Have you met anyone?" "How is Melinda?" She described herself as closing in on seventy with a bad heart, everything sagging and sporting a new hip. The surgery had kept her in the hospital two days longer than necessary because she hadn't come out of the anesthesia well.

"I don't think I'll let them put me under again," Aunt Lucy wrote in a somber tone, unlike her usual cheerful letters. "The physical therapy is difficult, and I get tired so easily. I can't seem to keep up these days. Now that I'm a widow and the kids are grown, this house is too big for one person." But the letter ended with the happy announcement of a second grandchild and a promise to write again at Christmas. He folded the letter and put it back in the card, tapping the envelope on his knee as he let his mind wander.

The last time he had seen Aunt Lucy was when his mother had died twenty years earlier. She was as different from her younger sister as black from white. He remembered the day clearly. It had been a bright, sunny morning and had fit his mood perfectly.

"Hank, dear, Come back to New York with me," she urged after the funeral. "You need to be near family."

Henry smiled but politely declined. "I have a good job in Chicago. Melinda got me a position at the museum."

Aunt Lucy had rolled her eyes and grinned. "There are bigger and better museums in New York, you know."

"I like this museum."

"So you two are still together?"

"No. Not like that. We're just friends." Henry waited for the "I told you so" he would have heard from his mother.

"That's too bad. She's a nice girl." Aunt Lucy squeezed his arm, her round face full of sympathy. "It's nice that you can stay friends, though. 'A good friend is hard to find' my husband always says."

"Yes, ma'am," he answered, thankful she didn't pry.

"Well, you're only twenty-three. There's plenty of time to find someone." She gave him a big hug and patted his back. "Are you still painting, Hank?"

"Yes, ma'am."

"Good. You always had a talent for that." Aunt Lucy nodded and gave him a wink, her blue eyes sparkling. "I'm glad you never listened to your mother. She was my sister but she was wrong, you know, about a lot of things."

Henry had shrugged but was secretly delighted to hear someone say those words. No one would have dared spoken such things when his mother was alive—except Aunt Lucy. She was the only one who'd never been intimidated by her.

"How is that fancy lawyer husband of yours?" Henry asked with a mischievous grin.

"You sound just like your mother. She always said I ran off to Detroit to catch a rich man," Lucille replied as she pinched her nephew's cheek. "Maybe she was right. Maybe she'd have been nicer if I'd stayed and helped with the business."

Henry had grown up in St. Joseph, a quaint, little tourist town along the shores of Lake Michigan. The residents catered to the artsy city folk who wanted to escape the commotion of Chicago. His parents ran a boarding house that had been in his mother's family since the Depression. A couple of hours drive from Chicago, the sandy beaches and small town charm of St. Joseph and its sister city, Benton Harbor, were popular vacation destinations.

With hard work and a prime location on the lake, his mother had turned the boarding house into a lucrative business. It was known for being clean, reasonably priced with a good, hearty breakfast included in the lodging fee. This made it an ideal place for young couples and families on a budget trying to beat the oppressive city heat without breaking their bank accounts.

Henry, who seldom received a kind word from his mother, had always been amazed how different she sounded in front of the "paying customers." She went above and beyond for those strangers with a smile on her face. Henry would have given anything to have that unfamiliar smile aimed at him.

"The woman could find a way to criticize the Lord, Himself," his father used to say. He avoided his domineering wife with a second job running the carousel at the public beach.

"Putting in extra hours with the bottle is more like it,"

she'd say with a sneer.

Henry picked up the slack at home. He missed out on Saturday afternoon baseball games, Sunday matinees, and bonfires on the beach. He waved at the school kids through the window of the ice cream shop but never stopped in. By the time it dawned on him that his sacrifices would never win him that smile his mother reserved for customers, it was too late. He no longer felt comfortable with kids his own age. The thought of walking up to a group of classmates and joining in a conversation terrified him. So, he stopped trying to please her, stopped trying to fit in, and concentrated on survival.

Then one day when Henry was ten, he visited a local art boutique on an errand for one of the boarders. His life was never the same after he walked through that door. The owner had smiled knowingly at the awestruck look in the boy's eyes as he took in the artwork. Henry became a regular visitor, and before the end of the summer was doing odd jobs around the shop in exchange for art supplies and sketching lessons. At first, he worried his mother's demands might ruin his chance to explore his interest in art. But Mr. Blasey never minded rescheduling an appointment when "something came up." Henry would always be grateful for the kind man's friendship.

His painting became the ultimate escape from an unhappy world. When his mother made him feel small, he would go to his room and paint something larger than life. Sometimes he painted himself as another person from another time. Sometimes he painted himself into an entirely different family. His imagination became his new best friend, and the paints were the toys they played with.

A knock on the door brought Henry back to the present. It would be Melinda. She was the only person who visited.

2

"I know you're in there, Hank. Let me in!" Melinda stood with her hands in her pockets resisting the urge to pick off the peeling paint on the door trim. She would never understand why he stayed in this godforsaken hole. But then she didn't understand why Hank did a lot of the things he did. She breathed a sigh of relief and ducked inside as soon as the door opened.

As always, the inside of his apartment took her breath away. She was in love with his work. The man could paint a cardboard box and make it come alive. Melinda had hounded him for years for an exhibit at her gallery, but he steadfastly refused. His reply was always the same. "My paintings are my life not my living."

"You got your hair cut." Of course, Henry noticed instantly.

"Yes. I told the my hairdresser I wanted to look younger. So she chopped it all off at the shoulders and gave me some highlights." Melinda pushed a stray wave off her forehead with a quick swipe of her hand. "What do you think?"

"Beautiful." Henry helped her off with her coat and hung it next to his own.

"Is this new, too?"

"Why, yes. Do you like it?" she asked, her hand lingering on the fur collar.

"That color looks good with your blonde hair. I should paint you in it."

"And where would I be?" Melinda asked impishly. "In an ice castle from Dr. Zhivago or the snow-peaked mountains of Colorado?"

"I'll take you anywhere you want to go."

"Sure—as long as you don't have to leave this apartment." She gave Henry a hug and smiled when he returned the squeeze. His cheek felt warm against her cold skin. "Someday I'm going to drag you out of here kicking. There is more to the world than St. Joseph's and your five-block radius to the museum."

"Not fair. I occasionally venture out to the theater, grocery stores, and a few choice restaurants that are outside my five block radius."

"Only because my daughter gives you the big, sad eyes and a pitiful 'Please, Uncle Hank?' It's almost embarrassing how Katie can twist you around her finger."

"Her little finger, at that." Hank laughed as he walked into the kitchen. "And I will travel someday, when I'm ready. But for now I'm content."

Melinda chewed on her bottom lip, arms crossed. "Is it enough?" she asked.

"Is what enough?"

"Being content? How about being so happy you're giddy or so miserable you can't stop crying?"

"You take care of the extremes and I'll keep the boat

steady," He opened a drawer and pulled out a bottle opener. "Red or white?"

"What are we eating?" The delicious aroma of comfort food filled the air when Hank lifted the lid of a crock-pot to give dinner a quick stir. "Roast with potatoes and carrots."

"Red." Melinda began her leisurely stroll around the large living room.

"Hank, you need a life outside of your canvases. You deserve a life of your own."

He smiled. "It's not as bleak as that." As she took the glass of wine from his hand, he tipped her chin up with a finger. "It's my life. Let me live in my own world in my own way. Please?"

She nodded and pretended to look through a stack of paintings. She'd tackle this subject later. "Anything new?"

"In other words, can you look at the easel? Yes."

Melinda peeked around the easel and gave a low whistle. "Who is this?"

"A woman I saw coming home from the museum last week. She had the sweetest smile. It stayed with me all the way home so I knew I had to paint her." Henry joined her in front of the easel.

"No background. Where will she be?"

"Don't know yet. It'll come to me." Henry put his arm around Melinda's shoulders and whispered in her ear. "I have something for you."

Those five words made her stomach jump with anticipation. "Really? A present? You know how I love presents."

Henry pushed her towards a Christmas scene tucked away on the corner windowsill. "Over here."

While the backgrounds in Henry's paintings were always detailed and beautifully done, the people were the focal point. Looking into the faces he recreated, she was immediately drawn into their world. Melinda knew that if Henry ever let her show his work publicly, he would become a prominent name in the art world. But he was stubborn and hated the idea of people gawking and criticizing his work.

Turning toward the painting, Melinda gasped. Off in one corner was the usual beautifully decorated tree with several brightly colored gifts underneath. The fireplace was decked out in the traditional Christmas finery, with a wreath centered above it and evergreen boughs and stockings hung on the mantel. But what drew her eye was the young woman next to the fireplace rocking her baby. The expression on her face was that of a new mother, the perfect combination of love and wonder.

"Oh, Hank, for me?" Melinda looked at Henry with tears in her eyes.

"Do you like it? I was going by memory. Your first Christmas with Katie was seventeen years ago."

"It's wonderful." She knelt in front of the portrait and traced the rocking chair, the child. "I was so frightened after he walked out on us. I had no idea how I was going to support the two of us on my measly salary."

"I knew you'd be fine." Henry squatted down behind her, kissing the top of her head. "You are one of the strongest women I know."

"I'd have never made it without you, Hank. If you hadn't given me those paintings to sell..."

"Then you'd have found another way to open your gallery and take care of your daughter. Besides, you got me my dream job at the museum."

Melinda reached for his hand on her shoulder and rubbed her cheek on the rough knuckles. "I wish you'd let me exhibit your work instead of selling a few here and there when you need the money. You could be rich, you know."

"You exaggerate my talent. When I'm gone, you can do whatever you want with my paintings. Until then, I hope you are happy with this one."

"This one will never be for sale. Thank you, Hank. Katie and I are so lucky to have you." Melinda wiped at her eyes. She wasn't in the habit of getting sentimental.

"Speaking of selling, I'll need you to act as broker for me again. You can send the money to the usual place." Standing, he held out his hand and helped Melinda to her feet.

"Your aunt? How is she getting along since her husband died?"

"She's a trooper. I think some unwise investments left her bank account a bit strained. And none of the kids are close by." Henry shrugged. "If you read between the lines, you can tell she needs some help."

"Why don't you go see her, Hank?"

"We've been through this before." They sat down on the couch that had cemented their friendship years before. Melinda thought he needed more furniture for guests and he insisted he wouldn't be having guests. She struck a bargain. If he had a sofa, she would come for dinner once a week. A furniture van arrived in front of his building two days later. Melinda arrived that evening with Chinese take-out. The ritual had continued for over twenty years.

"Let's change the subject. How is Katie doing with her college applications?" Henry knew it was a sore subject that could keep her ranting for hours. Her daughter wanted to attend college in California and Melinda could list one hundred and one reasons why Katie should stay closer to home.

The evening flew by, as it always did. It was ten o'clock before they knew it, and Melinda stifled a yawn.

"I hate seeing you so tired. You work too hard,"Hank said as he walked her to the door.

"It's my gallery. If I don't work hard no one else will." Melinda debated whether or not to bring up a taboo subject after such a relaxing evening. She put on her coat, and then suddenly spun to face him. "I want you to meet someone."

Henry shook his head. "Not this again. The last time was a disaster." "That was my fault—"

"I know it was." He tried giving her a stern look but ended up with a crooked grin instead. "Look, I know there is someone out there for me. Just let nature take its course, O.K.?"

Melinda shook her head. "Listen, my dear friend, no one will measure up to your lovely lady at the museum."

"That's not fair."

"You're absolutely right. It's not fair," Melinda said, her voice beginning to rise. She knew it was a losing battle but she was in too deep now. "You'll never find a real woman when you spend your lunch breaks and days off pining over an imaginary lover—"

"Enough!" The angry word hung silently between them.

Melinda saw the immediate regret in Hank's eyes as tears filled her own. Blowing out a loud breath, he held out his arms. She walked straight into them, her words muffled against his chest.

"You're such a good man, Hank. You should have someone to share your life with, have a family, the whole package."

"I'm sorry. I know you're only trying to help," Henry said as he held her tight.

He kissed the top of her head and stepped back. "I'd

settle for just love. But try to understand, I'm lonely, not miserable or pathetic." He chuckled. "Maybe I'll get a cat."

"Good God, a cat!" Feeling better, Melinda dropped the subject, for now. "By the way, what about Thanksgiving? I'd love to have my two favorite beaus with me for the start of the holiday season."

"So it's getting serious with Dave?"

Melinda felt herself blush and let out a sigh. "I think he's the one, Hank."

"I'm happy for you."

"Please, come for Thanksgiving. Katie insists on making pumpkin pie from scratch." They both rolled their eyes and laughed. Melinda's daughter was infamous for her disastrous attempts in the kitchen.

"And I get to be the guinea pig?"

"Who else would risk chronic indigestion?" "Or worse. Of course, I'll be there."

Against her usual protests, Henry walked her down to the street and waited until she was safely in a cab. As he watched the taillights fade away, Henry wondered where he would be if he hadn't met Melinda. The thought caused a shudder as he slowly made his way back up the stairs. She had been his savior, his way out of St. Joseph and his mother's boarding house.

Melinda had been working as a scout for an art gallery in Chicago. Her boss had stopped through the little vacation area on his way to Detroit. He was impressed with some of the local pieces displayed in the area shops and restaurants. So Melinda was sent to dig up some new talent.

Fortunately, for Henry, her boss was cheap and Melinda

ended up with a room in his boarding house. That Sunday she had wandered upstairs and stumbled upon his room, and his motley collection of paintings, had been the luckiest day of his life.

Henry fell for Melinda like an anchor hitting the water. She was like no one he had ever met before and treated him as if he were—somebody. Her enthusiasm and passion were contagious. By the end of the week, he packed up his life's work, followed her to Chicago, and never looked back. He had fancied himself in love with her but it turned out to be infatuation. Not with Melinda, but with her beauty and zest for life. While their affair had been short-lived, the friendship had endured.

Tackling the dinner dishes in the kitchen, Henry found the silence weighing down on him. He turned on the radio and heard the sound of a familiar Christmas tune. "It's beginning to look a lot like Christmas..." He hummed along. The commercial Christmas season was officially open in Chicago. While others mumbled about Thanksgiving being practically passed over, Henry reveled in the whole gaudy display. He loved Christmas and everything it entailed. It had been the only happy time in his house while growing up, thanks to Aunt Lucy.

Every year, she arrived the weekend before Christmas and left the day after New Year's. Lucille would laugh at all of her younger sisters' protests and put the family through all kinds of "holiday hell" as his mother used to call it. Lucy would drag Henry and his father up to the attic and pull out all the Christmas decorations and lights. The three of them would cut down a tree after extensive arguments over the perfect pine. The scent of evergreen still brought a smile.

For days, there would be singing and laughter and happiness. That one week in December would get him through the whole year. It was a time when Henry could pretend his family was like any other. Even his mother smiled, letting out an occasional rusty laugh. But it was the quiet evening talks with Aunt Lucy he loved most.

They would sit on the couch together and gaze out the picture window at the imposing white caps on Lake Michigan. The reflection of the Christmas lights on the window made it look as if there were strings of electric buoys floating in the water. Aunt Lucy would blow at the tree and watch the silver strands of tinsel gently sway and twinkle, taking on the color of the closest bulb. They would talk about their hopes and dreams and she would tell him about life outside the boarding house and St. Joseph, Michigan.

When she put her arm around his shoulders and kissed him on top of his head, he knew it was story time. Her tales were always about the magic of Christmas Eve.

"It's the one night of the year when your wishes really can come true, when anything is possible." Aunt Lucy was so sincere when she said this, Henry knew it must be so.

Years later, he concentrated on those happy holiday memories rather than the emptiness that would creep back each January 2 when Aunt Lucy returned to Detroit. And he refused to remember the devastating feeling of abandonment the year she married a lawyer from the firm where she worked. Shortly after, the annual Christmas visits stopped when her new husband relocated to New York City.

Henry hated New York City.

"Hey there, Henry." The security guard greeted him with a smile. "Snowing out there yet?"

"Nope, no snow yet but you can feel it in the air." Henry took off his overcoat and put it in his locker before turning to look at the row of monitor screens. "How's it going, George?"

"Another quiet evening." The guard chuckled. "Watched a movie with my kids that made me think of you. It was about a night watchman in a museum like the Field. The place came to life at night – wax figures, dinosaurs, everything. It was hilarious. You see it?"

Henry shook his head. "No, but it sounds a lot more exciting than this place."

"I'll let you borrow the DVD sometime." He buttoned up his coat and pulled on his gloves. "G'night, Henry."

"Goodnight, George."

Henry checked all the monitors again before starting his rounds through the museum. His painting wasn't on the radar. The portrait by the unknown artist had been hung in an obscure corridor out of courtesy. Henry often wondered whether that was part of her attraction. Rounding the corner, his eyes locked onto Rebecca. It never ceased to amaze him how she could look so lovely and tragic at the same time.

"Hello, Rebecca. Just making my rounds. I'll be back on my break." He knew if anyone overheard him, they'd think he was crazy.

But Henry had convinced himself that he talked to her because it was so quiet at night. And by directing his conversation at something, he wouldn't be talking to himself. It wasn't as if he was delusional and thought she was alive.

At break time, Henry took his sandwich and a folding chair to Rebecca's corner. He told her about the Thanksgiving dinner coming up and Katie's plans to attempt a homemade pumpkin pie. Remembering the movie George had told him about, Henry explained the plot.

"There's a security guard working the night shift in a museum." He spread his hands out. "Yeah, I know, sounds familiar. Anyway, it's a fantasy flick and everything in the museum comes alive at night. It sounds crazy—"

Henry froze. He could have sworn he'd seen the slightest smile on her face. His half-eaten sandwich forgotten, eyes squinting in concentration, he watched Rebecca intently for any signs of movement. *Maybe I am delusional.* He shook his head and returned his attention to the ham and cheese.

Several nights later, Hank studied her with a wary eye. That half- smile now haunted him in his sleep. Why did the painting have to have such a desolate backdrop? The artist could have added touches of color here and there to relieve the harshness. Had it been a punishment?

"I would never have put you in a setting like this for eternity. Did he hate you so much?" As Henry heard himself ask the question, his hands went to his face, palms rubbing tired eyes. Good grief, what was happening to him? He shook his head and let out a ragged breath. *Whoa, there, Hank. Your imagination's working overtime.*

As he finished his lunch, Henry continued to study the painting. One thing he knew for sure: All life forms in art were based on something known or seen by the artist. This woman had existed somewhere, at some time. Who was she? When had she lived? Or was she still alive? It was impossible to place her in a time period from her dress. The mystery made her all the more alluring. Was it sadness in her look or just loneliness? He understood the latter.

"What if I just added a few wildflowers, right here?" Henry pointed to Rebecca's knees. "Just a little pop of color to boost your spirits." Would he see that fleeting smile again, he wondered? As he turned to leave, he felt some-thing—like a cool puff of air across his face. Odd. The heat was always kept at an even temperature and there were no windows or doors nearby for a breeze.

Backing away, he tipped his hat. "Until tomorrow night, my dear. Perhaps, I'll bring you a surprise."

3

H ank was so intent on his plan, he couldn't sleep. He finally got up and tried to paint but it was a rainy day and the light wasn't good. When he looked at the canvas, he could only see Rebecca and that bleak background. The patter of rain and insistent ticking of the clock invaded his thoughts. It grated on his nerves, so he turned on the radio.

Bing Crosby's voice filled the room. "I'll be home for Christmas. You can count on me..." Hank smiled and thought of Aunt Lucy. The Christmas tune soothed his restlessness, as he got ready for work. By ten o'clock, he was putting on his coat and heading out the door.

Lugging the oversized shopping bag up the wide stairs of the museum, he stopped to swipe his key and punch in the security code. Henry's heart beat faster as he looked up at the dark building. He sucked in the cold, November air and watched his breath come out in small, white clouds of smoke. Oh, how he loved this time of year. Call it intuition, but somehow he knew this holiday was going to be very special.

He began singing to himself as he walked inside.

"Christmas Eve will find me... Where the love light gleams... I'll be home for Christmas—" Hank stopped at the door of the surveillance room. George would know something was up if he didn't wipe the stupid grin off his face. Trying to look serious, he opened the door and stepped into the quiet room.

"A bit early, aren't ya, Henry?" asked George.

"Yeah—there wasn't much on television so I just came on in." Henry tried to appear nonchalant though his insides hummed with excitement.

"I meant the Christmas stuff," George laughed, nodding to the paper bag.

Henry plunked it down on a chair and shrugged. "I was cleaning out the back closet and found some old decorations. I figured we could use a little cheer."

"Dang! Not even Thanksgiving yet." There was a tense moment as George poked at the wreath and gold garland stuffed in the top of the sack.

"Oh, that. Jeez, I've been watching the commercials since before Halloween. I can wait if you want me to..."

"Nah, go ahead. You're right, this place needs a little sprucing up." George headed over to his locker. "You care if I sneak out of here a little early?"

"Be my guest." Henry hoped he didn't sound too eager. "Anything to report?"

"Same ol', same ol'." George put on his coat and pulled his gloves out of his pocket. "Thanks, Henry. G'night, now."

Henry watched the monitors until George left the building. He took the Christmas decorations out of the bag and laid them on the counter. Taking a deep breath, he pulled out the soft leather bag that held his painting supplies.

What was he thinking? What if he got caught? He could lose his job. But if he was right... This was the most daring stunt he'd ever pulled. Heck, who was he kidding? This was the only stunt he'd ever pulled.

Henry whistled softly to himself as he finished his rounds. Stopping at the surveillance room, he grabbed his sandwich and Coke in one hand and the satchel in the other and headed down the hall. By the time Rebecca came into view, he had almost talked himself out of the whole ridiculous scheme.

But when he gazed up at her, all reason flew out the window. He had been looking at this woman for twenty years. Now suddenly she was pulling and tugging at his heart. Or maybe, not so suddenly. Perhaps his obsession was actually her calling to him, and he was afraid to listen.

"Well, Rebecca. Let's see what we can do for you tonight." Henry's heart pounded as he went to work mixing just a few colors—a little green, a little yellow and white. He spoke low and soft as he began to paint. His tone was gentle and soothing.

"I snuck all this in under some old Christmas decorations. I'll have to hide everything in my locker until after New Year's." Pausing, he looked up. "I wonder if you like Christmas? It's the only holiday I look forward to."

Within moments, two tiny buttercups blended into the landscape, their leaves just touching the woman's knees. Hank stepped back and examined his artwork. He doubted if anyone would notice the change. Except him and Rebecca. "What do you think, beautiful? Like it?"

His stomach clenched. He swore her head moved in an imperceptible nod of approval. Wiping his hands on a rag, he peered closely at the painting. "Is this what you want, Rebecca? Does this help?" Hank stood for several minutes willing her to move or make a sound.

With a deep sigh, he bent to pick up his satchel and

again felt that soft burst of cool air on his neck and the subtle smell of...salt. Yes, like a faint ocean breeze. Hank's common sense told him to be alarmed but as he turned back, his heart was filled with an overwhelming need to comfort this woman.

"I have to go now. I still have to decorate the monitors or George will wonder why I hauled in all that junk." He smiled at her tenderly, suddenly feeling very protective over this image he had known for so long. "Okay, here's the deal. If no one pays any attention to us, I'll add more color in a couple of days."

And he did. The changes made to an unremarkable painting were overlooked. No one noticed the embellishments of an insignificant painter. And Henry was thrilled. Within a month, the woman on the cliff was sitting amongst a patch of wildflowers.

And only the security guard on the night shift saw a transformation in the woman. The haunted look had been replaced with a more serene expression. She no longer seemed to be searching for something. Instead, she seemed to be waiting for something. Henry was determined to figure out what it was. And when he did, it would be the best Christmas gift he had ever received.

As the days passed, Hank felt like a new man. He sent his first Christmas card. Oh, to be a fly on the wall when Aunt Lucy received her hand-painted yuletide greetings from Chicago! She'd think he'd lost his mind. Maybe he had, he thought with a mischievous grin.

Nights at the museum took on a new urgency. He had to finish by Christmas. It was his gift to himself. He calculated the finishing touches should be done by Christmas, and rubbed his hands in anticipation. Anticipation of what? Hell, he didn't care. He had a mission. In the back of his mind, a little voice threatened his exuberance. *What will you do when it's complete? What will you have to look forward to then?*

Tuning out the niggling question, he focused on the present. He would enjoy this bit of happiness thrown his way. Just like Aunt Lucy's holiday visits. If sorrow and heartache came afterwards, then so be it. Rebecca was more than worth it.

The telephone jangled, interrupting his thoughts.

"Hello there, stranger." Melinda's familiar voice came through the receiver. "Haven't seen you since Thanksgiving. Did Katie's pie scare you off?"

Henry chuckled. "I was only sick for three days. But I'm fine now. Tell Katie I'll be her taste tester anytime."

"So, how many Thursdays are you going to cancel on me?"

"To be fair, my dear, you cancelled the first time. Threw me over for a date with Dave and his parents, if I recall."

"Are you punishing me or just jealous?"

"Neither. You know I'm happy for you."

"So why do I feel like you're avoiding me?"

"I've been putting in some extra hours at work. I'm the only one without a family here so..." He hated lying, but Melinda knew him too well. If he spent any time with her at all, she'd get him to spill his guts and think he'd finally gone off the deep end. Besides, a gallery owner would not appreciate tampering with art pieces.

"I'm worried about you, Hank. Anything you want to talk about?" Silence. "Okay, next subject. What are you doing for Christmas? I promised Katie we'd visit my brother in Wisconsin. Why don't you come with us? We're going up Christmas Eve and only staying the night."

"Sounds great but I have to work Christmas. And I have a date for Christmas Eve."

"What? Finally—I mean, really? When did you meet her, and why haven't you given me details? Do I know her?"

"Don't get too excited," Hank warned. "I'm planning a quiet evening with an old friend. Yes, you know her. And that's all I'm saying for now."

Melinda sounded ecstatic. "You couldn't give me a better gift, Hank. I'm so happy for you."

After finalizing plans to celebrate Christmas a day late, Melinda made one more attempt to get more information about his date. With a wicked chuckle, Hank hung up the phone. Poor Melinda. Her mind would be spinning with possibilities, mentally going over anyone they had come in contact with over the last twenty years. That should keep her busy for a while!

"Happy holidays, Henry. The wife made the traditional raisin bread." George handed him a loaf of brown bread wrapped in plastic wrap with a red bow on top. "About ten seconds a slice in the microwave with a little butter on top and it'll melt in your mouth. It's my favorite."

"Why thanks, George." Henry was touched. He fumbled in the pocket of his overcoat. "I brought back that movie. You were right. It was pretty good."

"Thought you'd appreciate the storyline." George slapped him on the back. "Got plans for tomorrow?"

"No, the day after. Going to a friend's for dinner." Henry gave an over-exaggerated grimace. "Her daughter is attempting homemade bread pudding."

"Not the creator of the sugarless pumpkin pie."

"One and the same."

"Well, I'd gladly trade places with you. Kids are out of school next

week, the in-laws are here and my wife makes me use vacation time. Probably won't see ya, so Happy New Year."

Henry laughed. "You don't know how lucky you are, George. Happy New Year to you, too."

Henry took a deep breath and sat down trying to focus on the monitors. But tonight he had only one thought. *It's Christmas Eve.*

He peeled open the plastic wrap and tore off a hunk of the brown bread. It was delicious without butter or a microwave, which was good, since in his excitement he'd forgotten to pack a lunch.

His rounds seemed to take forever. Finally, he headed down the hall toward his usual haunt. Rounding the corner, he stopped and sucked in his breath. She was exquisite. He allowed himself a few moments to study her from a distance. He had to admit this was his best work.

The whole painting was absolutely stunning. The rigid cliff and dramatic shoreline were a striking contrast to the splashes of color surrounding a breathtakingly beautiful woman. The dim sky was now a darkened blue that matched the sapphire of her eyes. Rebecca's smiling face was turned slightly, as if she were looking at something just beyond the frame. Her smiling face...

Frowning, he slowly approached the canvas, spotting changes he had not made. Henry had only added to the setting. He had never touched a brush to Rebecca. Yet, she was smiling. His gaze wandered from her face and saw her arm was in a different position. Her hand, no longer in her lap, reached for something. Or someone, Henry realized with a jolt.

He felt a gentle breeze on his face as the smell of salt again invaded his senses. "This is it, Rebecca." Henry's voice was soft, caressing. He looked at that empty palm and wondered what her skin would feel like.

"Is there anything in particular you want before I finish?" A painting was not for a lifetime, but for eternity. He hoped with all his heart he had done enough to keep her happy for that long. "It's Christmas Eve, you know, the most magical night of the year. A night when anything is possible."

In the end, Henry decided not to add another stroke. The painting was perfect. Falling into his nightly routine, he spoke again of his aunt and the Christmas card he'd sent and of Melinda's determination to discover his mystery date. He sat with her well past his usual lunch break. He felt foolish, waiting there, hoping for some kind of sign. But, dammit, this could not have been just his imagination. There was a bond between them—a reason he was drawn to her.

He could almost taste the disappointment. He had hoped that, for the first time in his life, something extraordinary would happen to him. Reluctantly, he rose to leave. Looking up at her, he sighed, reconciling himself to another bittersweet holiday. "I just wish..."

Henry's shoulders slumped. The exuberance that had propelled him throughout the past weeks trickled away, leaving him hollow inside. He had been prepared for the hurt, but not this emptiness. It was worse than any pain he could have imagined. Henry suddenly felt very tired. And rejected.

Walking up to the painting, he looked directly at her. "I have loved you from the moment I laid eyes on you. I will love you all of my life. Merry Christmas, Rebecca."

As he slowly turned to walk away, he heard a whisper. "Merry Christmas, Henry."

Melinda tried his apartment for the third time and again got his voicemail. It was three o'clock and he was over an hour late.

"It's not like Uncle Hank to be late, Mom. Maybe we should go over there." Katie's face mirrored her mother's concern.

"You stay here in case he calls," Melinda said as she grabbed her coat. "I'll phone you as soon as I know something."

She was at Hank's apartment within half an hour. No one answered her knock or the frantic pounding and yelling. "Hank. Hank. Please, answer the door."

Fingers of dread tickled her spine, as her mind raced with all the horrible "what ifs" threatening her composure. The building manager finally appeared to find out what the ruckus was about and quickly got a key to open the door.

The apartment looked the same. Nothing was amiss and she found no clues to Hank's disappearance. She sat down on the threadbare couch she had bought him twenty years before and started making the dreaded hospital calls.

When she had no luck, Melinda phoned Katie. "I don't suppose you've heard from him?"

"No." Her voice broke. "Mom? What are we going to do?"

"Well, at least he's not in a hospital." Melinda pushed back the panic. "I'm heading over to the museum to see if he showed up for work last night. I'll call you back as soon as I know anything. Call me if you hear from him."

The mystery deepened after talking with the guard.

"There was some bread left on the counter and his coat thrown over the chair, but no sign of Henry." The old man shrugged. "I called George, the second shift guard. He said everything was fine when he left Christmas Eve."

Which meant Henry had to be somewhere in the museum. A heart attack? He was barely forty, but it had happened to younger men. If he had fallen, he would have yelled for help. Unless he was unconscious. What if he'd finally given up and actually...?

Bits of conversation bounced around in her head. "*I might have a date myself...*" "*An old friend...*" "*Yes, you know her...*"

Of course! Breaking into a run, she headed for his favorite spot in the museum. Melinda found the usually deserted hallway filled with a small crowd of patrons. Henry's beloved painting had never received any notice at all, but was now the center of attention.

A uniform jacket was lying crumpled on the floor in a corner. *Henry!* She grabbed it, searching it for some clue. And found a piece of paper stuffed in a pocket. With unsteady hands, she opened the letter.

Dear Melinda,

Please take care of Aunt Lucy, the rest is yours. I have my masterpiece. Be happy for me.

Love, Henry

Melinda's heart raced, each beat pounding in her head, as she turned to look at the painting. It was magnificent. A woman sat on the edge of a cliff, surrounded by flowers, the wind blowing her dress and auburn hair. Standing over her was a man, strong, dark and handsome. He held her small hand in his, gazing down at her as if she was the most precious thing on earth. The expression on their faces caught her attention, held her captive. If she didn't know what love looked like, she had only to glance at this painting.

On the canvas, Melinda saw the face of her best friend and the woman he had been waiting for all of his life. Henry was fine. Better than fine, he was home. She had never felt such pure, utter joy for someone.

As she listened to the comments from the crowd, Melinda was filled with awe. She finally got it. She finally got *him*. His previous paintings had been a prelude to this journey. Henry the Insignificant had created something remarkable. That was more than most people accomplished in a lifetime. And along the way, he had found love. Oh, how he deserved that, Melinda thought, as tears welled up in her eyes.

With a tremulous smile, Melinda nodded at her friend from behind the group of admirers. "Merry Christmas, Henry. Way to go."

Reviews are an author's life blood. If you enjoyed Merry Christmas, Henry please consider leaving a comment at your favorite retailer.

The Chicago romance books are all standalone stories. Get Dante's Gift, a contemporary romance that includes a special WWII romance.

AUTHOR'S NOTE

I hope you enjoyed this holiday fantasy short story. This is my very first published work and will always hold a special place in my heart. Although I often add a touch of magic to my stories, this is the only time the reader does not experience the physical closeness of both main characters.

I've been asked if Henry's story might continue and learn Rebecca's tale. Truthfully, I have attempted it several times but I have not been able to expand to the plot without it seeming forced. So I leave you with my little holiday twilight zone story and hope it brings you some Christmas joy.

ABOUT THE AUTHOR

About the Author

USA Today Bestselling author Aubrey Wynne resides in the Midwest with her husband, dogs, horses, mule, and barn cats. Obsessions include wine, history, travel, trail riding, and all things Christmas. Her Chicago Christmas and Regency series have received multiple awards and nominated numerous times as a Rone finalist by InD'tale Magazine.

Often loosely based on family and friends, her contemporary romances take place in a small town south of Chicago where she taught for twenty years. The setting of Dante's Gift was brought to life by her stepfather who served in North Africa and Italy during WWII. Paper Love and For the Love of Laura Beth were inspired by real-life couples.

Aubrey's first love is medieval romance but after dipping her toe in the Regency period in 2018 with the *Wicked Earls' Club,* she was smitten. This inspired her spin-off series *Once Upon a Widow*. In 2020, she launched the Scottish Regency series *A MacNaughton Castle Romance* with Dragonblade Novels. Her Regency detective series, *Paddy's Peelers*, will launch early 2024.

Website: http://www.aubreywynne.com/

Subscribe to Aubrey's newsletter for new releases, exclusive excerpts, and free stories:

Newsletter: http://www.subscribepage.com/k3f1z5

Facebook Reading Group: https://www.facebook.com/groups/AubreyWynnesEverAfters/

SNEAK PEEK: DANTE'S GIFT

Chapter One

Love is friendship that has caught fire. It is quiet understanding, mutual confidence, sharing, and forgiving. It is loyalty through good and bad times. It settles for less than perfection and makes allowances for human weaknesses.

— ANNE LANDERS

The piles of discarded clothes resembled the glorious Chicago skyline at dusk. The deep sunset colors cluttered the floor and the bed, as Katie James systematically emptied out the huge walk-in closet. She shook her head in frustration each time she gazed at the mirror in a new outfit.

This was *the* night. The night Dominic would pull a dazzling ring from his pocket and ask her to become his wife. He had been like a kid with a big secret for the past three weeks: distracted, smiling for no apparent reason, and cracking stale jokes. All sure signs that he plotted with the "happy gods." Several times when she'd texted or called, he told her he was Christmas shopping. Ha! No man bought holiday gifts in October. He said to dress up because he had something special planned. There could be only one explanation—a proposal.

Looking out the window from her Lake Point Tower condo, she watched the sailboats bob in Lake Michigan and played out the evening in her mind. Dominic would be dressed in a tailored suit that hugged his wide shoulders. His long fingers would betray his nervousness as they combed through his thick, dark wavy hair. She would shiver delicately when those smoky eyes caressed her face. He would reach for her hand—

Good grief, get a hold of yourself. This is real life not some sappy chick flick.

Jasmine, her best friend, plopped onto the couch. "What are you wearing tonight? I came to give my approval. I have a better sense of romance than you."

"What's that supposed to mean?"

Her friend snorted. "You create ledgers while I create romantic allusion."

"True, I could use another opinion. My room looks like a tornado hit it. I'll pour you a glass of Merlot and put on a fashion show."

An hour later, both women stood in front of the full-length mirror with huge grins. Katie turned from side to side, watching the vibrant jade dress sway under the black silk jacket. A hint of cleavage peeked out from the scooped neckline. "You are brilliant. I would have never put this together."

"That's why I design clothes and you add numbers. See how the darker colors showcase that deep auburn hair?" Jazzy said as she arranged the mass of waves into a loose chignon, leaving long curls to frame her oval face. "I wish you would show more leg, but this is subtly sexy. Now where are the green topaz earrings and pendant your parents bought you last Christmas? They're the exact color of your eyes."

An hour later, after a professional make-up session, she gave her friend a hug. "Good luck tonight. I hope it's everything you have dreamed of since we were girls."

Katie laughed. "No, you hope it's everything *you* have dreamed of since we were young. "

"Same thing. I admit I always thought I'd find my soul mate first, though."

She rolled her eyes. "You know I don't believe in that. Love, yes. True love, love at first sight, fate? No. Compatibility, similar backgrounds and interests, friendship—those are the things that determine lasting love."

"Yeah, yeah, yeah. But you can't tell me your stomach never flips when he looks at you a certain way, or your legs get wobbly during a particularly passionate kiss." Jazzy waggled her finger and ignored the second roll of eyes. "Now remember to get at least a little teary-eyed when he pops the question. Pinch yourself if you have to but let him know how much this means to you. We both know you're lousy at saying what you feel."

"You make me sound like a cold fish," she said with frown. "I don't ooze emotion but I can show affection. Besides, I didn't have much practice in my family."

"When was the last time you gave me a hug?"

"Just now." Katie bit her lip, knowing what was next.

"No, I hugged you. There's a difference. I'll get off my soapbox if you promise to try to make tonight as special for Dom as he is making it for you. Throw sensibility to the wind and kiss him in public." She headed for the door. "And for god's sake, don't forget to tell him you love him. He should not have to take it for granted when he puts a ring on your finger."

"Time out! I promise to wear my heart on my sleeve and follow all the rules of Miss Jasmine's School of Romance, if you promise to leave now," she agreed and pushed her friend toward the door. "Go pretend you hate Thomas and leave me in peace. I'll call you first thing in the morning."

"Call me from the bathroom afterwards. I want to know all the details."

Katie shut the door. From the other side came a muffled, "And text me a picture of the ring."

A few minutes later, Vivaldi's Four Seasons played on her cell phone. Dom's handsome face smiled up at her, and she quickly swiped the screen. "Hey there. Not cancelling on me, are you?"

"Not a chance. Finished up the week's orders and cleared some days on next month's calendar." He paused then continued in a low, caressing tone, "I miss you, Kathleen James. It's been a week since I've held you in my arms. No more extended business trips if you want me to remain a gentleman."

Her pulse raced as his deep voice flowed through her like a rich cup of coffee. "Don't threaten me, Mr. Lawrence. You're the one working twelve-hour days. Besides," she added, getting into the spirit of the game, "maybe I like an old-fashioned rogue once a in awhile."

The moan on the other end made her chuckle. "Are you still picking me up at seven?"

"What time is it now?"

"Grrr. It's six-fifty." She tapped her foot on the hard wood floor. "You're late again, aren't you?"

"Is that your toe making a staccato beat? I-am-ir-ri-ta-ted. Why-can't-he-be-on-time." She could hear the grin in his tone. *Sense of humor, check.*

"You took the words right out of my—" A knock at the door. "Hang on a minute, okay?"

Not expecting anyone, she looked through the peephole. A charcoal-grey eye stared back at her. She quickly opened the door.

"Boo!" He held out a bouquet of white and pink flowers.

The aroma of white roses and star lily gazers filled the room. *Thoughtful, check.* Then he pulled her close, nibbling at her lips as her arms went around his neck. When the kiss deepened, the flowers fell to the floor. Katie leaned into him, allowing his strong hands to hold her up.

Strong and sexy. Check.

***

Dominic pulled up in front of the unassuming brick building and waited for her reaction. It had taken him months to set up this evening. The head chef, with three Michelin stars and countless James Beard awards to back him, drove a hard bargain. The extra truffles he had agreed to provide would be worth the private corner and the "added extras" by the staff. The valet approached the car and he watched Kathleen's shrewd eyes take in the scenery.

"No way. You have tickets to dine at Alinea's?" She shook her head. "Do you know how much—"

He put a finger on her mouth, then brushed the long, red curls from her cheek and put his lips in their place. "You are so beautiful... let me spoil you tonight without one word about the price."

She smiled and kissed him back, her lips soft against his skin, then wiped her lipstick print off with her thumb. The valet opened the door and he ducked his head as he climbed out of the silver Lexus. He walked around to the other side and assisted his beautiful date onto the sidewalk.

The restaurant, tucked away on Halsted, occupied what had once been a residential brickstone. They entered a long, darkened hallway strewn with hay and pumpkins for the season and passed a very busy kitchen. He tightened his grip on Katie's arm before she gravitated toward the commotion and smells. A pleasant younger woman greeted them and escorted them upstairs to a secluded corner.

"I didn't expect this décor to be so minimal. I imagined a few priceless paintings on the wall or chandeliers." She nodded in approval at the sand-colored walls with dried arrangements of reds and yellow and oranges for accents. "I love it."

Dom explained, "Most people expect lavish because of their reputation, but the philosophy is to focus your attention solely on the food." A waiter appeared with the first wine selection. "And the beverages." He gave his approval for the first bottle by a slight incline of his head.

With the first course of shrimp, clams in their shells, and seaweed, the server asked to imagine a beach; the small shrimp washing ashore among the seaweed and seashells. Dominic could almost hear the ocean.

The next two hours produced a display of mesmerizing dishes with a production and story to accompany each course. He stopped counting after ten and lost himself in the experience. The gorgeous redhead next to him lit up with each new presentation and kept her promise. She never once brought up the $600-$800 plates.

During a hot potato-cold potato course, the waiter leaned down and said softly, "The head chef said he is especially pleased with the black truffles. He hopes you will come again soon."

"Tell him if he has done his job, I won't need a return visit." He looked over at Katie, her green eyes dark with excitement and cheeks flushed from the wine.

A sharp pang of worry threatened the moment. He'd hit a small snag in his plans and knew he had to tell Katie about Nonna first. It wouldn't be fair to let her say "yes" and then spring it on her. *Please, please, if anybody is up there listening, help a poor guy out!*

"Sweetheart, I had a surprise phone call this week..."

***

Katie pushed her forehead against the cool bathroom tile and took a deep, shaky breath. *What just happened? It was not supposed to go like this.* The perfect romantic night had turned into a disaster. *How can I go back out there and face him?*

She pulled away from the wall and stared at her reflection in the mirror. Tears glistened in her dark green eyes. One slipped down her cheek and onto the front of her silk jade dress. The dark stain slowly spread like the frustration that crept through her soul.

Dominic Lawrence was perfect. His dark, good looks, and tall, athletic body had women taking a second look whenever he entered the room. They had similar interests but were opposites in personality. He was easy going to her serious nature. She liked to plot and plan; he loved spur-of-the-moment. Her thriftiness made him chuckle. They accepted their differences and balanced one another. And the man could make her blood boil with a look or a touch.

Why now? Fumbling in her purse for her cell, she tried to put things in perspective. *Calm down. He might change his mind. She might not agree.* Katie swiped the screen, her finger slicing across the necks of the happy couple smiling back at her. *That's ironic.*

"Oh my god, you remembered to call me. Did he propose?" her best friend's voice gushed over the line. "Where did he take you?"

"Alinea's." She tried to stamp down the impatience she felt at Jazzy's enthusiasm. "Listen—"

"No way. It's one of the most expensive restaurants in Chicago. He had to buy the tickets months ago." Alinea's, a premiere restaurant on the east side, did not take reservations but sold tickets instead.

"I know. Now listen—"

"I heard they have a green apple helium balloon. It's clear and you put your mouth on it and suck in the flavor. Then the helium affects your voice... Are you crying?"

"No, yes. Oh Jazzy." She let loose a sob as another conversation didn't hit the mark. She felt as if she were in the twilight zone.

"Did he propose?" The excitement was gone from her friend's voice, replaced with concern and wariness.

"Not yet." She held the phone away from ear, anticipating the loud reprimand.

"WHAT? Where are you? The *bathroom*?"

"Yes, but I—"

"It's just a little panic attack. We practiced this. Your traditional

Italian man gets down on one knee. He says something so tender and sweet that you smile, get a little moisture in your eyes—"

"He wants to bring his grandmother back from Italy to live with him."

Silence. A speechless Jazzy would be laughable at any other time. "Help me." She hated the pleading in her tone, hated not being in control of a situation.

"Give me a minute, you caught me off guard."

Katie heard the snap of her fingers on the other end. She only did that when she was stumped. *Oh, god.* "What am I going to do? You know I'm not a demonstrative person."

A snort burst through the phone.

"I'm not like the rest of his family. They are in your face, hugging then fighting then hugging again. I need peace. And privacy. And personal space. What if she's like the New York branch?"

"You don't need space from your hunky Italian." Jazzy chuckled. "The Romano family is loud, affectionate and unfiltered. I adore them. But remember, there are dozens of them. Dominic was raised an only child like his father, who was raised by Antonia. His cousins are all on his mother's side."

"I've never met her but he's talked about her so much. His grandmother is all he has left on his father's side. What if she's a domineering matriarch? I can't even cook." She batted a wisp of hair from her eyes, mindless of the pins that threatened to fall from the loose bun. "Or worse, what if she's a decrepit old woman? I have a terrible bedside manner. Can you see me emptying bed pans or feeding someone?"

Laughter bubbled from the phone. "From the stories Dom has told us, she probably has more energy than you. Antonia sounds very independent and may refuse to come back with him."

Katie hadn't thought of that. Perhaps all this drama was premature. "That's a good point. But Dominic doesn't put his foot down often and when he does, he's impossible to sway. He says he owes his life to that woman."

Jazzy took on her let's-be-reasonable tone. "She came back for her son and daughter-in-law's funeral and stayed two years. According to his cousin, Dom would have walked away from the family business if his grandmother hadn't intervened. He owes her a lot."

The tears stung the back of her eyes again and she silently nodded her head. It was time to give back, and the man she loved would never turn his back on family.

"Do you love him?"

"With all my heart." The voice of reason. What would she do without Jazzy?

"Then you can't tell him no."

"But how can I tell him yes?"

Silence. Then a chuckle. "Okay, Plan B. Here's what we do…"

* * *

Dominic stared at the empty chair across from him. The whole evening was a catastrophe. He ran his fingers through his hair, sending the thick waves in uneven spikes.

He had planned this evening for six months. The Alinea staff knew him by name. Every detail checked and rechecked, so he only had to worry about stumbling over his own words. This night her eyes would glisten with emotion and their life together would begin. Dominic had left nothing to chance.

Or so he thought.

Yesterday he received a phone call from his grandmother in Italy. Her younger sister had passed away, and Nonna was now living alone at the age of eighty-eight. Insisting she was healthy and mobile, she had only called to let him know of the funeral arrangements. "I knew you would want to attend, and perhaps you could help me with some of the details," she had said then paused. "*Mi manchi*, Nico."

"I miss you too, Nonna," he had answered with a crack in his voice, feeling like a little boy again.

Now he looked at the vacant spot across from him. When he'd told Katie that he wanted to bring his grandmother back with him, it was as if he'd thrown a cold, wet blanket on their fire. She had sat quietly while he tried to explain, make her understand his need to care for his grandmother himself. Then she nodded, murmured an excuse, and practically ran to the restroom.

I'm an idiot. I should have been subtler, led up to it more. But in the end, it didn't matter what Katie thought. He couldn't let Nonna live alone at her age. She had always been there for him. And regardless of the sacrifice, he would be there for her.

He pulled his cell phone from his pocket, scrolled down, and touched Vince's name. *Deep breath, call the man who always has an answer.*

"Hey, Dom. Well, is it official?" His cousin's voice boomed through the tiny speaker and put a grin on his face. In the background, he could hear the chatter of several women and his uncle competing to be heard.

"There's been a slight hitch."

"He's getting hitched, Ma." A muffled cheer then Vince added, "Ma wants you on speaker phone."

"No, wait. I haven't—"

"Dommi, your mamma would be so happy and your papa so proud," gushed his Aunt Maria. "We need that Skip thing so we can kiss you through the screen. Kathleen is a lucky girl."

"Zia, you don't understand. I haven't asked her yet."

"*Perche no?* What is taking you so long?" She began making shushing noises at his cousins. He could almost see her arm flapping at the three youngest girls, Bianca, Bella, and Gemma.

"Congratulations, Dommi," yelled the twelve-year-old Gemma.

"We love you."

"Give Katie a big hug from us," added the teenage twins, Bianca and Bella.

"Zia Maria, I need to talk to Vince." His fingers clutched the phone and he tried to keep his voice down. He glanced at the closest table but they had gone through several bottles of wine and had their own show going on.

His uncle's voice bellowed over the racket. "Why are you calling us then? Did she stand you up?"

Dominic ran a hand over his eyes. "No, Zio Tony. She's in the bathroom. Now let me talk to Vince."

"You're calling us while she takes a potty break? Vincenzo, take a lesson from your cousin on what *not* to do when you get engaged. In my day, a man..."

He heard a click and the voices faded slightly. "Sorry, Dom. I had to retreat to the roof." The sound of Brooklyn traffic somehow calmed his nerves after the speaker chat with Vincenzo's family. "What's up? It's your big night, bro. That chef has bled you dry with special orders, promising a night to remember."

Lawrence Produce and Supply catered to the high-end restaurants of Chicago. If black truffles were in short supply, his business found them. Vince traveled around the world to wheel, deal, and woo international export traders for the delicacies wanted by Michelin star chefs. Dominic sold them to the highest bidder. Or gave them away to have in exchange for the most memorable night of Katie's life.

"He's living up to his reputation and his promise. That's not the problem." Dom looked nervously at the doorway, not wanting to be caught on the phone. "It's Nonna."

"Nonna's there?"

Air escaped his lungs and his cheeks puffed out as he gave himself a face palm. "No, she called a couple days ago, remember?"

"Of course, how is she doing since her sister died?"

"Fine. But I hear the strain in her voice. I'm going to Italy for the funeral and bringing her back."

"Yeah, we figured as much. So Katie's not so happy, huh?"

"She practically ran for the bathroom. I'm afraid she won't marry me now." There, he'd said it out loud. The elephant in the room was now stomping all over their $1000 meal. "I don't think I can live without her."

"You couldn't live with *yourself* if you didn't help your grandmother."

A quiet pause, then Vince said quietly, "You know we'd be happy to have her here with us. She might like Brooklyn. With just the three girls left, there's plenty of room."

Dominic smiled and nodded his head. "I know you would. But she'll either come with me or stay in Italy. The only two places she has ever called home has been Benevento or Chicago."

"The way I see it, if Katie can't accept that then she's not the girl you thought she was. Better to find out now than later."

Deep down, he knew Vince might be right. But he also hated the timing. If they had been married, and Katie had already grown to love his grandmother, perhaps the look of panic might not have covered her face.

"Yeah, well. Thanks for putting things in perspective. I'd better let you go. She should be back soon." He ended the call and replaced the cell in his jacket pocket. Katie walked toward him, her red-rimmed eyes downcast.

He stood and pulled back her chair, leaning down to place a kiss on her cheek. As he sat down across from her, he reached out to hold her hand. "This is not the conversation I had planned for this evening, but I needed to be honest with you."

"I've never even met her. " She pulled her fingers back from his grip and placed her hands in her lap; her eyes remained down, telling him that she was systematically processing the information. "So, you haven't actually discussed this with your grandmother yet, correct? When do you leave?"

"Monday." In a typical Italian gesture, his hands shot out as he tried to explain, "If you just get to her know her. You'll love her as much as I do."

Out of the corner of his eye, he saw the maître'd move. *No. Not yet. That wasn't the sign.*

He watched Katie's chest rise and fall with several deep breaths; her eyes finally lifted to hold his gaze. "Why don't we wait and see what happens, okay? I'm sure we can work this out. She may even turn you down."

He opened his mouth to reply but two waiters appeared at the table and laid down a large cement plate. One dropped a spoonful of creamy chocolate here, lemon and orange there, while the other splashed arcs of colorful sauces and syrups, making it look like a wall of graffiti. As the men completed their artwork, Katie peered closely at the plate.

In the middle of the edible artwork, she whispered the words "Marry Me" aloud. Instead of a look of joy, he saw hesitation. His stomach clenched as he rose from his chair and knelt before her. Holding out a black velvet box with a simple princess-cut diamond ring, he took a deep breath.

"Kathleen James, you are the love of my life. Will you marry me and let me spend the rest of my years making you happy?" A drop of sweat rolled down his back; he steadied his hand. *Keep it together. You have a fifty-fifty shot now.*

Her eyes glittered as her hand flew to her mouth. For a moment, he thought she would run. Instead, she did something totally out of character.

She leaned down, placed her palms on his cheeks, and kissed him tenderly. His heart pounded at this rare public show of affection. He had his answer. Then her hands covered his and slowly pushed down until the box closed.

A single tear slid down her cheek. "I do love you, Dominic Lawrence. But I need more time before you ask me this again."

Other Contemporary Romance by Aubrey Wynne

A Chicago Christmas: Small Town Romance

Merry Christmas, Henry (A Chicago Christmas #1)

Preditors and Editors Readers Choice, N.N. Light Best Short Story Award

"Captivating Christmas Choice!"

Kindle Book Review

"Short, sweet, and stunning!"

Great Reads

Henry, a shy and talented artist, moonlights as a security guard at a museum and loses his heart to a beautiful, melancholy woman in a painting. As his obsession grows, he finds a kindred soul who helps him in his search for happiness. On Christmas Eve, Henry dares to take a chance on love and fulfill his dream.

Dante's Gift (A Chicago Christmas #2)

Winner of the RWA Golden Quill, Aspen Gold, and Heart of Excellence

Rone finalist, InD'tale Magazine

"Wynne has crafted a a beautiful short story guaranteed to warm your heart and make you sigh."

Kishan Paul, Second Wife *Series*

"...a wonderfully poignant holiday romantic tale that intertwines two love stories..."

Jersey Girls Book Reviews

"A lovely sweet romance!"

Book Addicts

Kathleen James has put her practical side away for once and looks forward to the perfect romantic evening: an intimate dinner with the man of her dreams—and an engagement ring. She is not prepared to hear that he wants to bring his grandmother back from Italy to live with him.

Dominic Lawrence has planned this marriage proposal for six months. Nothing can go wrong— until his Nonna calls. Now he must interrupt the tenderest night of Katie's life with the news that another woman will be under their roof.

When Antonia's sister dies, she finds herself longing to be back in the states. An Italian wartime bride from the '40s, she knows how precious love can be. Can her own story of an American soldier and a very special collie once again bring two hearts together at Christmas?

Paper Love (A Chicago Christmas #3)

Bragg Medallion recipient, Winner of Gayle Wilson Award for Excellence

Recommended by InD'Tale magazine

"This author has a knack for love stories that make your heart flutter."

Reads2Love Book Reviews

"Aubrey Wynne is a talented author weaving a descriptive setting, cultural details, historical facts, and inspirational romance into a delightful read."

Renate, Goodreads Review

Growing up in a Papua New Guinea mission, Joss Palmateer is a gentle soul with a unique view of life. Still adjusting to a new home in the U.S and the sudden loss of her mother, love is the last thing on her mind.

Sexy physical therapist, Ben Montgomery, meets his sister's friend and the sparks fly. He takes it as a silent challenge when she ignores his advances, but it's her extraordinary inner beauty that captures his heart.

With the help of a stray homing pigeon and an old origami legend, Ben sets an unwavering course of romance to win her love.

For the Love of Laura Beth (A Chicago Christmas #4)

Rone Finalist, InD'tale Magazine

Finalist for Best Book Buyers, The Maggie and The Beverly awards

"Beautifully written and tells a story that will allow readers to experience the turmoil that war can bring to the lives of those who must endure its heartbreak."

Verified Review

"This isn't your typical boy-meets-girl-they-get-married-and-live-happily-ever-after-the-end story. This is sweet romance in the midst of real life hardships and pain, and a love that will press through and triumph."

The Korean War destroyed their plans, but the battle at home may shatter their hearts...

Laura Beth Walters fell in love with Joe McCall when she was six years old. Now she is counting the days until Joey graduates from college so they can marry and begin their life together. But the Korean War rips their neatly laid plans to shreds. Instead of a college fraternity, Joey joins a platoon. Laura Beth trades a traditional wedding for a quick trip to the courthouse.

The couple endure the hardship of separation, but the true battle is faced when Joey returns from the war. Their marriage is soon tested beyond endurance. Laura must find a way to accept the tragedy thrown in their path or lose the love that has kept them anchored for so long. With a determination that only comes from the heart, Joe relentlessly fights an invisible enemy...for the love of Laura Beth.

Small Town Romance series

Saving Grace (A Small Town Romance #1)

Finalist for the The Maggie and Holt awards

"This unique piece has the reader traveling between the early 1700s and the early 2000s with ease and amazement. The audience truly feels sorrow for Grace and Chloe and is able to connect with each woman for the hardships they are overcoming. The attention to historical facts and details leave one breathless especially upon learning the people from the past did exist and the memorial erected still stands."

InD'Tale Magazine

"I enjoyed the way the book went from past to present really pulling the read in. The mystery was a delight. The author gives a wonderful story of two women fighting to keep what is theirs, showing their strength, love and courage to put one foot in front of the other while the world around them goes crazy."

Cyn, Top 500 Reviewer

A tortured soul meets a shattered heart...

Chloe Hicks' life consisted of an egocentric ex-husband, a pile of bills, and an equine business in foreclosure until a fire destroys the stable and her beloved ranch horse. What little hope she has left is smashed after the marshal suspects arson. She escapes the accusing eyes of her hometown, but not the memories and melancholy.

Jackson Hahn, Virginia Beach's local historian, has his eyes on the mysterious new woman in town. When she enters his office, he is struck by her haunting beauty and the raw pain in her eyes. Her descriptions of the odd events happening in her bungalow pique his curiosity.

The sexy historian distracts Chloe with the legend of a woman wrongly accused of witchcraft. She is drawn to the story and the similarities of events that plagued their lives. Perhaps the past can help heal the present. But danger lurks in the shadows...

Just for Sh*#$ and Giggles series

To Cast A Cliche (A Just for Sh*#$ and Giggles Short Story #1)

"...a fractured fairy tale with humor and tongue in cheek...to use a cliché."

Verified Reviewer

"Fairy tale lovers will delight in this short story... It's a fun read that will have you playing "count the cliches" until the cows come home."

Reads2Love

The evil Queen Lucinda exacts revenge on a royal poet by casting a spell of never-ending clichés upon the kingdom. Will the clever King Richard thwart his stepmother's magic and save the good people of Maxim? Test your literary knowledge and enjoy an entertaining spoof on fairytales.

Pete's Mighty Purty Privies (A Just for Sh*#$ and Giggles Short Story #2)

Preditor's and Editors Readers Choice Award

Goodread's Top 100 Laugh Out Loud List

"The author has a gift for clarity and humor and I can't recommend this short story   enough. Hilarious!"

N.N. Light Book Reviews

"Expertly written and hysterical. You can't go wrong with this one."

Renea Mason, The Good Doctor *trilogy*

Pete McNutt needs customers for his new business. Spring has arrived and it's prime time Privy Season. After much consideration, he refines his sales pitch and heads to the monthly meeting of the Women's Library Association.